How To Conquer the Tri-State Area

By Heinz Doofenshmirtz

Based on the series created by Dan Povenmire & Jeff "Swampy" Marsh

Disney XD

DISNEP PRESS
New York

Text by Ellie O'Ryan and Dan Povenmire

Printed in the United States of America

First Edition
1 3 5 7 9 10 8 6 4 2
J689-1817-10274
Library of Congress Catalog Card Number on file.
ISBN 978-1-4231-3465-7

For more Disney Press fun, visit www.disneybooks.com
Visit DisneyChannel.com

The *VERY EVIL* Table of *EVIL* Contents

DO you lay awake at night, hearing a little voice deep inside you say, "Am I as evil as I could possibly be?" Do you dream of a time when the mere mention of your name strikes fear in the hearts, minds, and even the small intestines of anyone who hears it? Excellent. Good for you. So . . . how's that working out so far? Need some help? Well, you're in luck! Because I, Dr. Heinz Doofenshmirtz, the most *evil* genius in the entire Tri-State Area, have prepared this manual to help you realize your evil potential. I personally guarantee* that after reading and perhaps *memorizing* this book, your capacity for dastardly deeds will increase by a minimum of five percent!

So, what are you waiting for? Turn the page and let's get started. And remember . . .

Today is the first day of the rest of your evil life!

* Some restrictions apply. Individual results may vary. Guarantee not legally binding.

Perhaps you're asking yourself, "Hey, this Doofenshmirtz fellow has impeccable taste and unparalleled style—but what does he know about evil? What can *he* possibly teach *me*?" If so, congratulations on your cynical nature and overblown self-confidence—these are excellent traits for an evil mastermind! Allow me to present my resume:

D.E. Inc

Doofenshmirtz Evil, Incorporated

As the president and founder of Doofenshmirtz Evil, Incorporated, it is my mission to spread evil throughout the entire Tri-State Area. Check out my *very* evil experiences so far!

Bratwurst Street Vendor

I was proud to sell Doofenshmirtz's Quality Bratwurst, with our superior workmanship, fine meats, and exotic spices. But when hot-dog vendors forced me out of business, I was filled with bitterness . . . and inspired to dedicate my life to the pursuit of evil!

Aspiring Magician

My experience with magic tricks has been invaluable training for building traps and creating inventions of doom!

Carnival Worker/Dunk Booth

I wasn't the guy who got dunked. I was what was thrown at the bull's-eye. It was a horrible job—but it showed me how evil the world could be. So that was good.

Before you travel into the twisted mind of an evil genius, I suggest you take this quiz to determine your personal capacity for evil deeds.

HOW EVIL ARE YOU?

1. When you eat a banana, what do you do with the peel?

   a) Throw it in the trash, of course!

   b) Eat it.

   c) Carefully place it on the ground, then hide in the bushes and hope someone slips on it.

2. When you watch a movie, you always want:

   a) The hero to win.

   b) The villain to win.

   c) More popcorn.

3. When you were a child, you really wanted:

   a) A bike, so you could help deliver food to the elderly.

   b) A fuzzy bear named Schmoopy.

   c) To marry into money—and then use your vast wealth to wreak your petty vengeance on an unfair world!

4. What is your heart's most secret desire?

a) To bring about world peace.

b) To develop the powers of a minor superhero. Nothing too flashy—just a cape and maybe some kind of heat vision.

c) To become a millionaire by selling only three cups of hot chocolate! And then take over the entire Tri-State Area!

5. If I became an evil genius, the first thing I would do is:

a) Retire.

b) Buy a flock of doonkelberry bats.

c) Launch my own brand of cereal.

EVIL-O-METER

If you answered mostly a's: I'm sorry to say that you have almost no evil sensibilities. Quit wasting my time, you Goody Two-shoes!

If you answered mostly b's: Your interest in evil is less than inspiring. You need to put more passion in your evil plans if you expect to make a name for yourself as a first-class scoundrel.

If you answered mostly c's: Your cold heart is *so* evil, it's frightening. In fact, I'm a little scared of you already.

Now, before we go any further, you must ask yourself this essential question: Do I have an enemy? If the answer is no, put down this book and find an enemy immediately! Any self-respecting evil genius must have at least one nemesis whose only goal in life is to foil his plans. I have compiled this gallery of known secret agents to get you started on your search.

GALLERY OF KNOWN SECRET AGENTS

CODE NAME: Agent P

NOTES: Perry the Platypus has been my number one nemesis since the very beginning. He has foiled just about every evil scheme I've ever dreamed of, so we're extremely well-matched.

CODE NAME: The *OTHER* Agent P

NOTES: He may look like a cute furry panda, but beware! He is *just* as sneaky as Agent P. (Which is why I call him the OTHER Agent P. Makes sense, doesn't it?)

CODE NAME: Agent H

NOTES: Without his hat, it's easy to mistake Agent H for an ordinary hedgehog. Let this be a lesson to you—always look for his hat!

CODE NAME: Agent C

NOTES: Agent C may *be* a chicken, but he's no chicken! What I am trying to say is that he is a literal chicken, but not a *figurative* one.

AGENT D

CODE NAME: Agent D

NOTES: This dog's bite is actually worse than his bark! He scares me, but only a little bit!

CODE NAME: Agent F, Agent F, and Agent F

NOTES: Don't let these fish fool you, they are *very* smart. (Maybe because they travel in schools. Get it? What, you're not laughing?)

AGENT F

AGENT F

AGENT F

CODE NAME: Agent K

NOTES: The *K* is for kitty. I have it on good authority that Agent K has petitioned to be called Agent C, but the real Agent C refuses to share his initial! Ha!

CODE NAME: Agent W

NOTES: Because of his small size, Agent W can *worm* his way out of all sorts of sticky situations. Har, har!

THESE AGENTS HAVE ESCAPED ME SO FAR, BUT THEIR TIME WILL COME!

My #1 Nemesis (Plus My #1 Creation!)

You can also use your enemy for inspiration. One time when my number one nemesis Agent P was *really* getting on my nerves, I made this list of ways to get rid of him forever!

1. Traps—too complicated
2. Giant tinfoil ball—too shiny
3. Automatic tennis-ball machine—too bouncy
4. Giant wad of chewed-up bubble gum—too sticky
5. Space helmet—too binding

Unfortunately, not a *single* idea was solid enough to eliminate Perry the Playtpus. So I decided to do a little research about platypuses, and I learned that the greatest enemy of the platypus is . . . man. Suddenly, I knew how to create the ultimate platypus-elimination weapon. All I needed to do was build a giant . . . killer . . . robot . . . man!

And without further ado, I would like to introduce to you my finest creation yet: **NORM!** I'm not *exactly* sure how Norm will eliminate Perry the Platypus. Perhaps Norm will pound him with his giant fists? Stomp him with his giant feet? Encroach on his woodland home with his ever-expanding real-estate developments? Whatever! That's between Norm and my nemesis Perry the Platypus. I promised myself I wouldn't get involved.

Now, let's take a moment to visit your past. The ordinary torments and miseries of childhood are full of evil inspiration! Allow me to share with you some examples from my own childhood. I grew up in a small town called Gimmelshtoomp. Ahhh, Gimmelshtoomp . . . I can almost smell the zotzenfruit. . . .

Spitzenhound Kennel

Gimmelshtoomp Carnival Grounds

Zotzenfruit Gardens

GIMMELSHTOOMP

Childhood: The Root of All Evil

When I think of the tender days of my youth, I remember when lean times came to the Doofenshmirtz family, and our beloved lawn gnome was repossessed. We were *devastated*. Who would protect our zotzenfruit garden from witches' spells and wood trolls? Well, my father decided that it would be . . . me! While the other children played Kick the Schtoompel and ate doonkelberries, I stood for hours as the spitzenhounds howled. My only companion was the moon—and my neighbor Kenny.

DON'T MAKE FUN OF ME. LAWN GNOME COSTUMES AREN'T FLATTERING ON <u>ANYONE</u>.

Since my lawn gnome was taken from me way back when, I decided to destroy every lawn gnome in the entire Tri-State Area! First, I collected all the lawn gnomes and hid them in my evil lair until I had a bounty of gnome riches. Then I tried to destroy them with my latest invention: **THE DESTRUCT-INATOR!** But wouldn't you know, Perry the Platypus came charging at me and caused me to pull the wrong lever, ruining my evil plan? Now I'll never get rid of these gnomes! Curse you, Perry the Platypus!

Like I explained on my resume, back before I was evil, I was something a little *less* than evil. I was a bratwurst street vendor, selling only the finest sausage—Doofenshmirtz's Quality Bratwurst!

But nobody remembers the dedicated bratwurst vendors of yesteryear. And why? Because of the hot-dog vendors! Oh, how I hated them. I was sure that it was only a matter of time before the public recognized the bratwurst's superior quality. But I was wrong, so to get my revenge I invented the **HOT-DOG REVENGE-INATOR!** It shot a Freon blast at an unsuspecting hot-dog vendor and made his weiners cold and soggy. Once I took the *hot* out of hot dogs, they were forced to sell my bratwurst instead!

You can also cultivate your evil genius to make up for the slights and insecurities of your childhood. That's why I created the BALL-GOWN-INATOR! When I was a child, my parents were expecting a baby girl. My mother spent months knitting pretty dresses. But, the baby turned out to be a boy, which turned out to be me. Since we were out of yarn, I was forced to wear those dresses for an entire year! I can still remember the mockery and scorn from all my manly classmates.

But now *I* have had the last laugh! It takes just one blast from the Ball-Gown-inator to instantly attire your enemy in a truly elegant ball gown. And now I feel much manlier, you know, by comparison. Look how *precious* Perry looks in his gown. Ha!

VANESSA DOOFENSHMIRTZ

This is my best friend, Balloony. I couldn't leave him out! (But more about him later!)

DR. HEINZ DOOFENSHMIRTZ

CHARLENE DOOFENSHMIRTZ

When you're finished mining your childhood for inspiration, it's time to look at the next most likely source: your family. If you are the latest descendant in a long line of evil geniuses, congratulations! How great for you . . . what more do you want—a prize? But if the rest of your family members are not that evil, don't despair. That's been my experience, and just look at me now!

FATHER DOOFENSHMIRTZ

MOTHER DOOFENSHMIRTZ

My father always loved his spitzenhounds more than me, and he forced me to be a lawn gnome. Come to think of it, he was a pretty evil guy, after all!

My mother meant well. She wouldn't have forced me to wear dresses if there had been any other option. Don't you think?

CHARLENE DOOFENSHMIRTZ

Charlene and I were married, but it just wasn't meant to be. We wanted different things. One of those things, for me at least, was to be evil.

ROGER DOOFENSHMIRTZ

DR. HEINZ DOOFENSHMIRTZ

My brother, Roger, the bane of my existence. He's just so *good* all the time! Ugh! Sickening!

The most evil Doofenshmirtz on the face of the planet: Yours truly!

VANESSA DOOFENSHMIRTZ

Sometimes my daughter, Vanessa, helps with my plots, but she doesn't seem interested in carrying on my evil legacy. I can only hope that one day she will yearn to become evil like me. A father can dream, right?

Now, let's take a break from all of this family talk. When you are a renowned evil genius such as myself, you will find that out of your *millions* of evil plans, a small number are so diabolical that they stand apart from the rest. And so, I am proud to present my **FIRST** very evil idea . . . the SOCKY SHOCKY SUITY!

You see, when I was a boy, my dearest friend was a balloon I got at a carnival. I drew a face on him, sprayed him with special lifelong-lasting spray, and named him Balloony. Then one tragic day, Balloony floated away. I tried to grab him, but it was too late. Balloony was gone. But I have never given up hope of finding him! Since balloons are drawn to static electricity, I invented the Socky Shocky Suity. All I have to do is charge it up, beam an amplified ray of pure static electricity into the air, and Balloony and I will be together once more!

Interesting footnote—it turns out that Balloony is now a turncoat named Colin who doesn't deserve the years of admittedly unhealthy obsession I have heaped upon his memory and . . . you know what? I don't want to talk about it.

Okay, now back to talking about my family. Oooh, how I loathe my Goody Two-shoes brother, Roger! I was so angry when Danville decided to give him the key to the city. But on the plus side, it inspired my **SECOND/ FIRST** Most Evil Idea Ever: the POOP-INATOR! (What, is this confusing? Have you never heard of more than one first idea before? Then you are not *truly* evil like me!) The Poop-inator can train pigeons to poop on just about anything. So when my brother accepts the key to the city, my pigeons will be ready to rain on his parade . . . with poop! Am I overexplaining this? Anyway, remember, my aspiring evil geniuses, that even the most mindless jealousy can lead to a truly petty act of vengeance!

ROGER DOOFENSHMIRTZ TO RECEIVE KEY TO THE CITY

LOCAL HERO ROGER DOOFENSHMIRTZ** will receive the key to the city of Danville today at Town Hall in recognition of his many kind and generous deeds.

Mr. Doofenshmirtz has rescued numerous kittens from trees, helped dozens of Danville's senior citizens cross the street, and purchased hundreds of cupcakes from the Fireside Girls. When asked about his status as Danville's favorite resident, Mr. Doofenshmirtz shrugged and said, "I don't think of myself as better than anyone else. I'm just better at doing things."

**He's a nice guy! Charming, too!

The DAILY DANVILLE   2

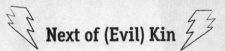

Next of (Evil) Kin

I thought having an evil daughter would help me, but usually it doesn't. I guess that's because she really isn't very evil at all! Once I had this amazingly evil idea to make a SPACE-LASER-INATOR that would destroy anything that annoyed me. Like that giant billboard that blocks my view. And nature—that is pretty annoying, too! And beauty! And morning talk-show hosts! Anyway, I was so excited about this plan that I even had professional blueprints drawn up. I asked my daughter, Vanessa, to go get them. Do you think she could handle one little job? Apparently not, because she brought me blueprints for some kind of giant ice-cream–sundae maker! What good is that to me? I'm lactose intolerant and can't even *eat* ice cream! My very own daughter foiled my plans! If she were truly evil she would have known better!

31

Evil Enemies

Well, that's enough about my family. Let's get back to talking about my enemies! Here is a valuable lesson: *never* underestimate a nemesis, no matter how slow, small, or inanimate he may appear. Not long ago, some dogs at the condo across the street were making an infernal racket, barking and howling at all hours of the day and night. So I baked up a gigantic dog biscuit and smothered it with irresistible gravy. I was hoping that all of the dogs would follow the **GIANT DOG-BISCUIT-INATOR**... right off the edge of the Tri-State Area!

Ah, to make a long story short, Perry the Platypus was a no-show, and I couldn't imagine being evil without a nemesis to witness it! So I put a hat on a plant and named him PLANTY THE POTTED PLANT. I really didn't expect much of a fight from Planty. Boy, was I wrong! He swung around on a rope and smacked me up and down my lair. With *fronds* like that, who needs enemies? Then a pack of crazed dogs burst into my lair and devoured my invention before I even had the chance to launch it! I'll get you next time, Planty! You are one fierce flora!

Okay, now back to my very favorite nemesis, Perry the Platypus. Even though he is my favorite, that doesn't mean I *enjoy* the way Perry the Platypus tries to ruin all my best plots. Once, I was so fed up with Perry that I decided I had to fight fire with fire. And by "fire," I mean Perry the Platypus, and by "fire" I also mean Perry the Platypus. So I invented the

PLATI-PROLIFERATOR-INATOR.

This amazing machine created dozens of doppelgängers to discredit and totally destroy Perry the Platypus! Such as Terry the Platypus and Larry the Platypus and Jerry the Platypus . . . I could go on, but you get the idea.

At last, I was *this close* to finally defeating Perry. But then Perry showed up and made the Plati-Proliferator-inator suck up all the doppelgängers. It exploded and scattered bits of platypus all over the Tri-State Area. How disgusting, right? Oh, Jerry the Platypus . . . I'll never forget you!

The Most *VERY* Evil Sleep Aides

When I think about how one day I will defeat Perry the Platypus, sometimes I get so happy that I can't fall asleep! Have you ever been so excited about your latest evil endeavor that you couldn't fall asleep either? That happens to me so often that I made a list of ways to fall asleep when all you really want to do is something terrible! After all, a good night's sleep is crucial if you want to perform at your most villainous capacity!

Ways to Fall Asleep

1. Count lawn gnomes.

2. Read a book. Have you ever read What Color is Your Evil Hot-Air Balloon? It's a great story.

3. Cuddle up with an evil teddy bear.

4. Obsess on a petty act of vengeance. (This is why I always keep a pad of paper on my bedside table.)

I know I won't be able to sleep a wink tonight, because I can't wait to unveil my **SECOND** Most Evil Idea Ever: the **MAGNETISM MAGNIFIER!** I am going to cover the entire eastern seaboard with tinfoil and buy the biggest magnet I can find. When I launch the Magnetism Magnifier, it will pull the east in a westerly direction, thereby reversing the rotation of the Earth! I'm not really sure what I will do then. Maybe buy a bunch of east-facing real estate and sell it again once it has a sunset view? Oh, well, it looks like I'm going to be up all night, so I've got plenty of time to figure it out!

It is very important for every evil genius to have an evil lair, a special place to call his or her own. I'm very proud of my lair, which is also the headquarters for Doofenshmirtz Evil, Incorporated.

HOW TO CREATE YOUR VERY OWN EVIL LAIR!

- Don't forget the potted plants for a homey touch! (Or in case you quickly need a nemesis!)

- You'll want to invest in a top-of-the-line blueprint-storage system.

- Leave lots of room for traps in which to catch your enemies.

- Make sure your tools and lasers are neatly organized.

- A walk-in closet for storing your lab coats is essential.

It's been my lifelong dream to open my very own school for evil! As you can see from this enormously enlightening book, I have so much to teach the world. And my dream is about to come true at last!

With campus locations in every local Laundromat across the Tri-State Area, students can learn the skills they'll need to succeed in only six weeks!

Earn a certificate in:

- Robot Building
- Chocolate Making
- Pigeon Watching
- Cheese Aging
- And many more!

Courses offered include:

- The Evil Things I Did Over My Summer Vacation
- Chain Letters: Your Partner in Evil
- Evil 102 (And you thought Evil 101 was evil!)
- A History of Evil
- And many more!

Enrollment begins now, so don't delay! Send your application to:

Dr. Heinz Doofenshmirtz
Doofenshmirtz Institute of Evilology
Danville, Tri-State Area

Please also include a 500-word essay on the theme "Evil: What It Means to Me."

I'm deeply distraught to report that the Doofenshmirtz Institute of Evilology (D.I.E.) is closed until further notice. It's a long story, too complicated to go into here. But in short: the entire school relied upon monkeys providing free laundry to the Tri-State Area. Then all the Laundromats would go out of business, providing prime real estate for satellite locations of the D.I.E. In fact, I invented my very unique, *truly* evil MONKEY-ENSLAVE-INATOR helmet to force monkeys to do the laundry. I figured I only needed to make one helmet—after all, monkey see, monkey do!

Well, even with the Monkey-Enslave-inator helmet, monkeys are terrible at doing laundry! Look at everything they did wrong in one day!

1. Too much starch!

2. Red socks mixed in with a white wash—everything turned pink!

3. An entire box of detergent in every load! Don't they know how expensive detergent is?

4. Banana peels in the dryer. Unforgivable! Who wants clean clothes that smell like burned bananas?

5. Who folds pants like this? Seriously!

Frankly, I think Perry the Platypus might have been involved in this debacle. He always foils my greatest plans!

Love (So Close to "Evil" Spelled Backwards!)

People are always surprised to find out that I consider love to be one of the most evil forces of all. Yes, love! Forget about flowers, hearts, and candy, and focus on the important stuff, such as jealousy. And revenge! And scorned suitors! There's nothing like love for inspiring great evil!

I didn't always feel that way. I used to be so tired of all those happy couples, mocking me with their happiness. So I invented the DE-LOVENATOR RAY to eliminate love in the Tri-State Area!

But then I met my evil soul mate! We had so much fun together:

Popping children's balloons . . .

Commanding a robot army . . .

Dropping water balloons on people . . .

We even dangled Perry the Platypus over a pond full of alligators!

Alas, the De-Lovenator Ray misfired and hit my dream girl, and she fell out of love with me—so our romance was ruined. Maybe I'm too hard on myself, but I can't help feeling at least partially responsible for the failure of this relationship.

My *VERY* Evil Appearance

Sometimes I think I would have more luck with the ladies if I were a little more . . . what are the kids calling it these days? Oh, right, handsome. I came up with some ideas to improve my appearance . . . but each one has a downside:

1. Exercise more. Oh, who am I kidding?

2. Wear a rubber mask . . . but that would make my ears sweat, and I hate sweaty ears!

3. Invent something to break every mirror in the Tri-State Area . . . not sure that will help me with the ladies . . . haven't really thought this one through.

4. Grow a magnificent beard and mustache to cover up my face . . . But I've tried everything, and I just can't grow really masculine facial hair.

I finally consulted my doctor. He said it was genetic, but I don't blame my parents. I blame everyone else in the Tri-State Area for being better looking than me. So I invented the **UGLY-INATOR!** It harnesses the horned frog's unpleasant appearance to render its target hideously ugly! Oh, I just can't wait to test it out on handsome movie actor Vance Ward. First Vance Ward . . . then the entire Tri-State Area! And finally, *I* will be the handsomest man in town, you know, by comparison. I will never get turned down for a date again!

As I mentioned before, I've tried and tried to grow facial hair—but nothing works. So I simply hate people with beards. It's just my luck that the city erected a statue of Rutherford B. Hayes, our nineteenth president, right next door. He's only the president with the best facial hair of all! There's no beard like a nineteenth-century beard. That horrible statue is a constant reminder of my follicular failure! Argh!

I had no choice but to invent the very evil BREAD-INATOR. Not only does the machine emit a ray to turn that statue into a loaf of whole-grain bread, it will also release a flock of hungry magpies to devour it. Beard go bye-bye!

Interesting side note: I created the Bread-inator by accident. I was actually trying to make a BEARD-inator! But when I was painting the label I got the letters mixed up, and it seemed like too much trouble to white it out and start over.

Now *this* plan is truly evil . . . so evil that it's my Most Evil Idea Ever number **THREE**! With the help of a trusty remote control, I will open the Danville Dam, flooding all the streets and creating beautiful waterways. But how will people get around, you ask? They'll have to buy my latest invention, of course!

It's like a car, but it can drive on the surface of water. I call it the **BUOYANCY-OPERATED AQUATIC TRANSPORT,** or **BO-AT,** for short. Everyone will want one! As soon as I press the button, we will move out of the automobile age . . . and usher in the age of the **BO-AT!**

Back to (Evil) Basics

Of course, when you're trying to come up with evil plots, you can always go back to basics. Nothing inspires me quite like the things I hate. And there are so *many* things to hate. It seems as if the Tri-State Area is just filled with objects I loathe!

1. Blinking traffic arrows. Stop blinking at me and telling me where to go! You are not the boss of me!

2. Ear hair. I've always hated you, ear hair!

3. Pelicans. Terrible creatures! What are you, a bird or a garbage disposal?

4. Musical instruments that start with the letter B. You know who you are, banjos and bagpipes and bongos. . . .

I could go on and on, but I'd run out of paper. So I invented the SHRINKSPHERIA! I just enter the name of something I hate, and the Shrinkspheria hones in on its molecular structure, turning its particles into sparticles and shrinking the object into a teeny, tiny speck so small I never have to see the object again! If that's not an example of evil genius, then I don't know what is!

Food (for Evil) Thought

Even though I hate many things, there are some things I do like—groceries, for instance! And even something as simple as your grocery list can be full of evil inspiration. Just take a look at mine!

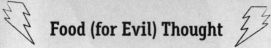

Limburger cheese

Capers

Pickled onions

Bratwurst—my favorite of all the wursts!

Beet skins

Hogburgers

Bean chips. Yes, you heard me correctly. Only non-evil people eat boring potato chips!

Mmm, I am drooling! Limburger is my favorite of all the stinky cheeses. In fact, I even gave up evil to pursue the art of cheese-making! I have an old Doofenshmirtz family recipe for Limburger cheese . . . but it has to age for fifty-eight and a half years. So I invented the **AGE-ACCELERATOR-INATOR** to make perfectly aged cheese. But my invention worked a little *too* well, and the cheese was so delicious that Perry the Platypus ate all of it! I was outraged! I created the Age-Accelerator-inator for peaceful, cheese-loving purposes, but Perry the Platypus forced me to wield it in anger! So my break from evil didn't last long after all.

HERE IS THE SECRET RECIPE FOR MY FAVORITE CHEESE SANDWICH— I JUST LOVE IT!

The Doofwich

Limburger cheese
Liver slices
Beet skins
Onion bread

Mustard
Pickle juice (Not an actual pickle. That would be gross!)

1. Layer slices of cheese, liver, and beet skins in a beautiful pattern on your onion bread.
2. Stir together the mustard and pickle juice and pour over the cheese.
3. Fight off hungry crowds as they try to steal your Doofwich!

I perfected this recipe when I was practically housebound due to one of my biggest pet peeves: people who dress as sandwiches to promote restaurants. I mean, what are you, a person or a food? Then I realized, why should I have to be a shut- in? So I invented the **SANDWICH-SUIT REMOVE-INATOR.** My creation is in the likeness of me—how evil! It sucks sandwich suits into the air and shreds them into teensy-*weensy* pieces. And once all the sandwich suits are gone, I'll never have to see another one. I hope Perry doesn't foil my plan!

Want to know what a really useful food is? Steak! Not only is it delicious, you can use it to heal a black eye, which is helpful when you find yourself battling a particularly persistent nemesis day in and day out. (I'm referring to you, Perry the Platypus.) That inspired me to invent the STEAK SPECS: glasses that hold raw steak on a black eye, leaving your hands free for evildoing. I stole all the steaks in the Tri-State Area so I could mass-produce Steak Specs and make millions!

Of course, Perry the Platypus showed up to ruin my plan. He set off my GIANT HEAT RAY, which I was saving for another evil plan, and now I have about a million laser-cooked steaks. What am I going to do with them? Serve fajitas to the entire Tri-State Area? That's not very evil. Invite Major Monogram over for dinner? I don't think so! Use them as roofing tiles? That would get pretty stinky in the hot sun. Curse you, Perry the Platypus!

Lately I have been eating way too many Fireside Girl cupcakes. And since I don't want to lose my girlish figure, I knew I had to come up with a plan—fast! I decided that the only thing to do was destroy the bridge from the cupcake factory to Danville. So I invented the **METAL DESTRUCT-INATOR**. It can turn any metal object into broccoli! Why broccoli? Because broccoli is healthy. It's like poetic justice . . . or, more accurately, poetic *evil*!

But *of course* Agent P turned the Metal Destruct-inator on itself, and now I have a mountain of broccoli florets to deal with. What am I going to do with all this greenery? Here are the ideas I've had so far:

1. Donate the broccoli to the Danville Elementary School cafeteria—no, that is too evil, even for me.

2. Invent a new musical style, "Broc-and-Roll," in which songs are played on musical instruments made out of broccoli.

3. Throw broccoli confetti on New Year's Eve . . . but I need to find a place to store the broccoli until December 31st.

4. Build a machine called the **BROC-INATOR** that will . . . I don't know. Something evil.

5. Eat all the broccoli myself until I reach my goal weight. . . . Let's hope it doesn't come to that!

Whenever I think about things I love (like Limburger cheese), I always think about . . . myself. When I discovered that my popularity had plummeted, however, I was very upset! Why don't people like me? Is it the whole *evil* thing?

Anyway, I want to remedy the situation immediately! What I'm going to do is create chocolate in my own image. Everybody loves chocolate! The **MELT-INATOR 6-5000** is powered by

thousands of laser pointers. All I have to do is aim the Melt-inator 6-5000 at the world's largest chocolate bar, and I will have more than enough chocolate to provide every resident of the Tri-State Area with a delicious chocolate Doofenshmirtz. What's not to love about *that* evil plan? If you decide to try this, be careful not to point your Melt-inator at something that can really make a mess, like marshmallows. That would be a gooey disaster!

My **FOURTH** Most Evil Idea Ever is one of my all-time favorites! I decided to create a mighty baby army! The BUM-BUM-INATOR will project the sound of my heartbeat across Danville. If my plan works, all of the babies in the Tri-State Area will believe that I am their leader, and then they will do my evil bidding! And no one will dare fight back against an army of babies, because they are *babies*!

This plan seems simple, but let me assure you that it's actually quite complicated. First, I will have to decorate an evil nursery for my baby army. And then I will have to invent the NANNY-INATOR, because *somebody's* got to change all those dirty diapers . . . and it's not going to be me. Then I will be ready to accommodate my mighty baby army. You know, this plan seems so well thought out and foolproof!

Stay Away, Evil Sunny Days!

Sometimes, no matter how evil you want to be, you just can't think of anything truly evil to do. Luckily, it doesn't happen to me that often, but that is because I am purely evil. But if you're *really* feeling low on inspiration, you can always turn to the weather. I mean, just look at this weather forecast!

WEATHER

M T W TH F

I hate perfect weather, because it makes everyone so cheerful and happy and carefree. It's a lot harder to take over the Tri-State Area when people are in great moods. That's where I got the idea for the GLOOM-INATOR-THREE-THOUSAND-INATOR! It will launch weather pellets into orbit and usher in a new ice age. People are always grumpy when it's gloomy . . . and soon it will be all gloom, all the time!

I had another idea that would harness the evil of cold weather for my own personal gain! This one involved quite a bit of start-up capital, as you can see from these receipts.

The Cocoa Hut
For all your chocolate needs!

Quality Powdered
Hot-Chocolate Packet $.50

Quantity: 10,000

TOTAL $5,000.00

HOT-DIGGITY DOG
Supplying Hot Dog Vendors for Over Fifty Years

Premium Vendor Cart
        $6,500.00

Quantity: 1

TOTAL $6,500.00

FREEZEFREE, INC.
Winter-weather gear for any season!

Purple Parka with
Faux-Fur Hood

Size: Medium $65.00

Red Flannel Long
Johns with Flap

Size: Medium $32.00

TOTAL $97.00

Well, nobody said that being an evil genius would come cheap. And the supplies will pay for themselves with my new plan... GIANT-ROBOTIC-PENGUIN-ICY-FREEZE-YOUR-SOCKS-OFF-BREATH-INATOR! After these giant penguins freeze the entire city of Danville, I will start selling my organic, yet highly

addictive, Doof-brand hot chocolate. Because who doesn't enjoy a nice cup of hot chocolate when it's cold out? The first cup will be free, of course. And the second will also be free. But then the third cup will cost a million dollars! That way I only have to sell three cups and I will already be a millionaire! It's pure evil genius!

The City of Danville Proudly Presents:

★ THE ANNUAL ★

MIDSUMMER'S FESTIVAL!

Rides, games, food, and fun for all!

THIS WEEKEND ONLY!

Can you believe this? That awful Midsummer's Festival is going to ruin my weekend! All that noise and traffic and laughing and music and the constant ringing of my doorbell by people who want to use my bathroom. With all this perfect summer weather, the festival is going to be packed!

But not for long. You see, I have discovered how to distill the smell of dirty diapers into a concentrated liquid form, which I will spread throughout the festival with my patented new invention, the amazing SMELL-INATOR! When the stink permeates the very molecules of Danville, the people will flee—and *I* will have all the peace and quiet I need to come up with a new evil scheme!

⚡ No News is Evil News! ⚡

Of course, if you *really* want to walk on the dark side, just take a look at the media. Everyone complains about the media, so it must be really, really bad! Which is why I invented the MEDIA ERASE-INATOR. See, the local news station kept broadcasting this *terrible* footage that made it look like I rescued a falling kitten. But it was just an accident! I mean, rescuing kittens is *definitely* not my thing. The timing couldn't be worse— the evil scientists' fraternity reunion is tonight—I have the invitation right here!

It's that time again . . .

EVIL SCIENTISTS' FRATERNITY REUNION

Join your evil brethren for a night of dinner and dancing . . . evil dancing, of course!

Awards will be given for the **MOST EVIL INVENTIONS** of the past year.

Don't miss it!

If the fraternity brothers see this footage, I will be a laughingstock. They might even take away my membership, and then I'd lose all my benefits! My reputation would be ruined! Luckily, the Media Erase-inator will erase all video signals, print ads, photographs, and images in the entire Tri-State Area—so I can attend the reunion without any embarrassment.

The latest terrible media outlet to anger me is *The Daily Danville* for refusing to print this obituary I wrote about my dearly departed creation, the evil GELATIN MONSTER.

IT IS WITH DEEP SORROW that we report the passing of the evil Gelatin Monster, which was destroyed during an unfortunate accident. The Gelatin Monster, which was only a few hours old, did not have much opportunity to prove how truly evil it was; however, during its brief life, the Gelatin Monster terrorized a group of children and even attempted to eat one. The Gelatin Monster is survived by its creator, Dr. Heinz Doofenshmirtz. In lieu of flowers, please send raspberry-flavored gelatin mix.

The accident that destroyed my Gelatin Monster also destroyed my TURN-EVERYTHING-EVIL-INATOR, which was how I made the gelatin monster evil! I always swore I'd never create the same evil invention twice, but now I am rethinking my position. If I had a new Turn-Everything-Evil-inator, not only could I create another evil Gelatin Monster, but I could make *The Daily Danville* more evil . . . if that's even possible!

Well, I think we've covered enough evilness for today! So . . . congratulations! You are more evil than evil. With the evil knowledge you have acquired, you will be able to defeat Perry the Platypus and all the other secret agents in the Tri-State Area! Hey, you are probably even qualified to graduate with top honors from the Doofenshmirtz Institute of Evilology. (Oh, wait, I think that school closed already.) In any case, you are an evil force to be reckoned with!

Now go get yourself a white lab coat and an awful haircut, because it is my pleasure to present you with this . . .

CERTIFICATE OF EVIL

By the evil power vested in me, Dr. Heinz Doofenshmirtz, I hereby proclaim that

———————————————————————————

NAME

(You write your name here, unless your name happens to be "Name" in which case you can just leave it the way it is.)

is now an official member of the League of Villainous Evildoers Maniacally United for Frightening Investments in Naughtiness (or L.O.V.E.M.U.F.F.I.N. for short. . . . We're working on the name, okay?)

WELCOME TO THE WORLD OF EVIL, MY FELLOW GENIUSES!